Ladybird  Readers

Little Survivors

Series Editor: Sorrel Pitts
Written by Cheryl Palin

LADYBIRD BOOKS

UK | USA | Canada | Ireland | Australia
India | New Zealand | South Africa

Ladybird Books is part of the Penguin Random House group of companies
whose addresses can be found at global.penguinrandomhouse.com.
www.penguin.co.uk   www.puffin.co.uk   www.ladybird.co.uk

Penguin
Random House
UK

First published 2018
001

Text copyright © Ladybird Books Ltd, 2018

Cover photograph and images on pages: 2; 5 (chipmunk, rattlesnake, grasshopper mouse, Harris hawk, great horned owl, centipede);
6 (wolf); 9 (chipmunk and grasshopper mouse), 10–33, 46 (chipmunk and grasshopper mouse); 47 (great horned owl, Harris hawk); 48;
49 (grasshopper mouse); 51 (wolf); 52; 54; 57; 61–62 (chipmunk and grasshopper mouse); 64 copyright © BBC, 2014.
Images on pages: 5 (sengi, monitor lizard, dung beetle, wildebeest); 9 (sengi); 34–45; 46 (sengi); 47 (monitor lizard); 49 (sengi);
50; 58; 59; 61–62 (sengi) copyright © BBC, 2014.
Image on page 6 (bear) copyright © Erik Mandre/Shutterstock.com.
Images on pages: 7; 51 (mountain lion) copyright © sumikophoto/Shutterstock.com.
Images on pages: 8; 51 (elephants) copyright © Andrew Linscott/Shutterstock.com.

BBC and BBC Earth (word marks and logos) are trade marks of the British Broadcasting Corporation and are used under licence.
BBC logo © BBC 1996. BBC Earth logo © 2014.

Printed in China

A CIP catalogue record for this book is available from the British Library

ISBN: 978-0-241-33614-4

All correspondence to:
Ladybird Books
Penguin Random House Children's
80 Strand, London WC2R 0RL

MIX
Paper from
responsible sources
FSC® C018179

Ladybird Readers

Little Survivors

Inspired by BBC Earth TV series and
developed with input from BBC Earth
natural history specialists

 To download full story audio in both British and American accents, and to complete
the listening activities at the back of the book, visit **www.ladybirdeducation.co.uk**

Contents

Picture words

chipmunk

rattlesnake

grasshopper mouse

Harris hawk

sengi

monitor lizard

great horned owl

dung beetle

centipede

wildebeest

CHAPTER ONE

Survivors of North America and Africa

Lots of wild animals live in North America. This part of the world has many different kinds of **habitats***.

The forests of North America change when the seasons change. These forests are home to big animals like bears and wolves.

bear

wolf

In the Sonoran Desert, in the south west of North America, it is very hot. It is also very dry, because it does not often rain. Many big animals live there, like mountain lions.

mountain lion

The African savanna has both a dry season and a rainy **season**, and it is home to some of the biggest animals in the world. Large groups of African elephants live here.

We often think of the big animals that live in these different places, but we should not forget that some **amazing** small animals live here, too!

African elephants

These little animals of North America and
Africa find amazing ways to **survive**.

chipmunk

grasshopper
mouse

sengi

CHAPTER TWO

In the Forest

It is fall in North America, and leaves and **acorns** are dropping from the trees in the forest.

One little animal is waiting for the acorns. He comes out of his **burrow** in the ground.

acorns

burrow

He is a very young chipmunk. He is only two months old, and fifteen centimeters tall.

The chipmunk has a clever way to take acorns to his burrow—he carries them in his **cheeks**!

The chipmunk is not going to eat the acorns now. He must save them in his burrow, because winter is coming. In the winter it is very cold, and chipmunks must stay in their **underground** burrows.

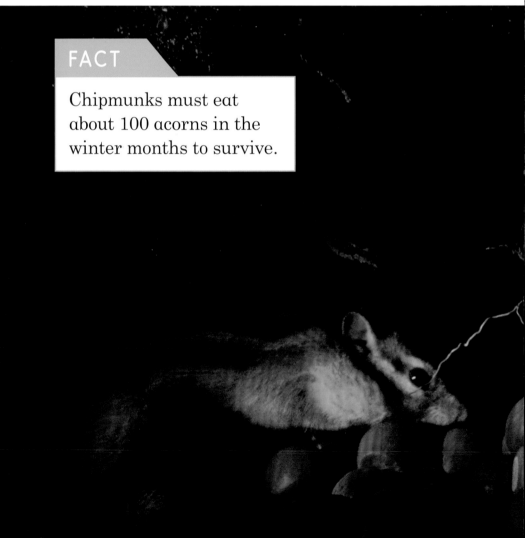

FACT

Chipmunks must eat about 100 acorns in the winter months to survive.

Big animals, like bears, **hibernate** in the winter, but a chipmunk cannot hibernate because its body is very small, and it must eat often to survive. It must have lots of food to eat in its burrow.

CHAPTER THREE

Problems for the Chipmunk

Other chipmunks in the forest must also find food. This older chipmunk is watching the young chipmunk very carefully as he collects acorns.

When the young chipmunk comes back, his burrow is empty. The older chipmunk has stolen the acorns! Without the acorns, the young chipmunk has no food for the winter.

This is not the only problem—the older chipmunk is hiding near the burrow! An older, stronger chipmunk can kill a young chipmunk. The young chipmunk is frightened, so he jumps out of his burrow and runs away.

Now, the young chipmunk must find more food—but not only chipmunks like acorns. This enormous moose is hungry for acorns, too. The small chipmunk must move fast to escape the moose's big feet!

moose

There are other dangers, too. In late fall, the days get shorter. Owls **hunt** in the dark forest at night.

FACT

The great horned owl is twenty times bigger than a chipmunk.

CHAPTER FOUR
Winter is Coming

At the end of fall, it gets colder.

The young chipmunk has escaped from the owl, but he must find food very quickly now. Soon, it will be too cold to look for food. Without food, the chipmunk will not survive.

The young chipmunk must find the older
chipmunk's burrow. He must find the
acorns that the older chipmunk stole,
and take them back!

When the young chipmunk discovers the
burrow, the older chipmunk is waiting . . .

The older chipmunk is bigger and stronger, but the young chipmunk must be brave. He has to fight.

Amazingly, the young chipmunk wins! He can take all the acorns back to his burrow.

The young chipmunk has lots of acorns now. He is safe and warm, and he can stay in his burrow until spring arrives.

Chapter Five

In the Desert

On the other side of North America is the Sonoran Desert. It is home to another little **survivor**—the grasshopper mouse.

When grasshopper mice are young, their mothers find food for them. Grasshopper mice sleep in the day, and come out at night.

grasshopper mice

A human can be killed by the venom in this scorpion's tail.

scorpion

Grasshopper mice are special, because they can eat food that other animals cannot eat. They eat **venomous** animals like scorpions, and the **venom** does not hurt them.

This young grasshopper mouse has left the **nest**. He is learning how to live, and how to look for food. He closes his eyes to **protect** them from this large centipede. He uses his **whiskers** to see.

centipede

whiskers

The grasshopper mouse is only three weeks old, and seven and a half centimeters long, but he can make a lot of noise! He makes a sound like a wolf to protect his home!

CHAPTER SIX

Problems for the Grasshopper Mouse

The desert is a dangerous place at night. There are more rattlesnakes here than anywhere else on Earth.

Rattlesnakes eat small animals like grasshopper mice. The young mouse must move very quickly to escape the hungry rattlesnake!

The weather can be dangerous for grasshopper mice, too. It does not often rain in the desert, but sometimes all the rain for one year can fall in one night.

If a grasshopper mouse becomes too cold and wet, it can die. When it rains, the little mouse must dry his **fur** very quickly.

fur

The ground in the desert is very dry and hard, so the rain water suddenly becomes a river.

The mouse has to run away from the fast-moving water, so he goes to another part of the desert. He is safe here, but he is far from home.

When the rain has stopped, the sun comes out and dries the desert quickly. Soon, it is very hot again. The hottest place is on the ground, where the grasshopper mouse is.

CHAPTER SEVEN

Danger for the Grasshopper Mouse

It is daytime. The mouse should be asleep, safe in his home, and he should not be in this part of the desert.

The biggest dangers to the grasshopper mouse are these Harris hawks, which are very clever birds.

Harris hawk

Harris hawks hunt in groups. Together, they fly after the grasshopper mouse.

Luckily, the mouse finds a safe place inside the **bones** of a dead animal. The birds cannot reach him here.

bones

The grasshopper mouse must hide inside the bones until night, when he can finally leave this strange place.

Then, this brave little survivor finds his way back home.

CHAPTER EIGHT

In the African Savanna

Far away, in another part of the world, is another little survivor. This is a baby sengi with her mother.

FACT

Sengis are sometimes called "elephant shrews", because they have long noses like an elephant's trunk.

Sengi babies hide while their mothers find food. The mother sengi runs along **trails** between the plants and grass on the ground. This small animal runs very fast to find food. She must eat so that she has milk for her baby.

Many small animals have to eat a lot. Sengis eat insects like **termites**. The mother finds a termites' nest, but there are not any termites here.

termite hole

Now, it's the home of a big monitor lizard!

The monitor lizard uses its **tongue** to smell the sengi. It knows that the sengi was here, and it knows where she has gone.

The mother sengi leads the monitor lizard away from her baby, but she does not survive.

CHAPTER NINE
Problems for the Sengi

Now, the baby sengi must learn to live by herself. Without her mother, she does not know which animals are friendly, and which animals are dangerous.

A young sengi must eat often. It is difficult to look for food in the long grass, but the sengi soon learns it is quicker to use the trails. She also learns to **clear** the trails.

It is important that the trails are **clear**, so the sengi can find food fast.

The sengi works hard, but there is a problem. Elephants often make the trails dirty again!

dung

The sengi cannot get past the elephant **dung**.

Luckily for the sengi, thousands of dung beetles arrive in minutes. These beetles make balls of dung, which they push away from the trail. The dung is food for the beetles and their families.

FACT

Dung beetles can smell dung from nearly a kilometer away!

dung ball

dung beetle

Chapter Ten

More Adventures for the Sengi

Down on the ground, it is difficult for a small animal to see when there is danger. Larger animals usually see the danger first.

These wildebeest suddenly begin to run because they are frightened.

The wildebeest have seen fire. Every year, there are large fires in the dry savanna. Sadly, many small animals do not survive.

The sengi can run fast to escape the fire, but she has to leave the trail.

After the fire, the savanna looks very different.

Luckily, the dry grass burned so quickly that the sengi trails have survived. The little sengi soon begins to clear the trails again.

Fires are not bad for the savanna, because new plants soon grow, and life will become normal again. Then, this little survivor can run around her trails and look for food again.

Chapter Eleven
Little Survivors

Chipmunks, grasshopper mice, and sengis all have to learn how to survive by themselves when they are very young. They must learn to find enough food to eat, and a safe place to live.

They must learn which animals are
safe, and which animals are dangerous.
They have to find clever ways to protect
themselves from the bigger animals that
want to eat them.

They also have to learn to live with other dangers, like the weather in their different habitats—cold winters in the forest, heavy rain in the desert, and fires in the savanna.

These animals are small, but they are also brave and clever. It is amazing how these little animals find ways to survive!

Activities

The activities at the back of this book help you to practice the following skills:

 Spelling and writing

Reading

Speaking

Listening

? Critical thinking

Preparation for the Cambridge Young Learners exams

1 **Read the text. Find the five mistakes, and write the correct sentences in your notebook. 📖 ✏️**

In the Sonoran Desert, in the south west of South America, it is very hot. It is also very dry, because it rains often. Many small animals live there, like mountain lions.

The African savanna has both a dry season and a rainy season, and it is home to some of the biggest animals in the world. Small groups of Indian elephants live here.

2 **Talk to a friend about these animals. Ask and answer questions. 💬**

wolf

mountain lion

African elephants

Which animal lives in the coldest place?

The wolf.

3 **Look at the picture and read the questions. Write the answers in your notebook.**

1 Where does the chipmunk live?

2 What does he eat?

3 How does he carry them to his burrow?

4 Why doesn't the chipmunk hibernate?

4 **Choose the correct words, and write the full sentences in your notebook.**

1 hibernate	hunt	protect
2 die	sleep	survive
3 acorns	insects	mice

1 Big animals, like bears, . . . in the winter, but a chipmunk cannot.

2 A chipmunk must eat often to . . . . It must have lots of food to eat in its burrow.

3 Chipmunks must eat about 100 . . . in the winter months to survive.

5 **Write sentences using _as_, _Now_, _so_, or _When_ in your notebook.** 📖 ✏️

1   This older chipmunk is watching the young chipmunk very carefully . . . he collects acorns.

2   . . . the young chipmunk comes back, his burrow is empty.

3   The young chipmunk is frightened, . . . he jumps out of his burrow and runs away.

4   . . . , the young chipmunk must find more food—but not only chipmunks like acorns.

6 **Read the sentences. If a sentence is not correct, write the correct sentence in your notebook.** 📖 ✏️

1   Moose like acorns, too.

2   The small chipmunk must move fast to escape the moose's big head!

3   In late fall, the days get longer.

4   Owls hunt in the dark forest at night.

5   The great horned owl is ten times bigger than a chipmunk.

7 Listen to Chapter Four. Answer the questions below in your notebook. 🎧*✏️

1 When does it get colder?

2 Why won't the chipmunk be able to find food?

3 What must the young chipmunk find and take back?

4 Where is the older chipmunk?

5 Who wins the fight?

8 Work with a friend. Talk about the two pictures. How are they different? 💬💬

 a

 b

In picture a, there are two chipmunks.

In picture b, there is only one chipmunk.

*To complete this activity, listen to track 5 of the audio download available at www.ladybirdeducation.co.uk

9 **Read the definitions of words from Chapter Five. Write the correct words.** 📖 ✏️

    1 someone or something that continues to live   s _ _ _ _ _ _ _

    2 a place where some animals live, made from sticks and dry grass   n _ _ _

    3 to stop anything bad happening to someone or something   p _ _ _ _ _ _

    4 something with venom in it   v _ _ _ _ _ _ _

10 **Match the two parts of the sentences. Write the full sentences in your notebook.** 📖 ✏️ ⭐

    1 When grasshopper mice are young,

    2 Grasshopper mice are special,

    3 Grasshopper mice eat venomous animals like scorpions,

    a and the venom does not hurt them.

    b because they can eat food that other animals cannot eat.

    c their mothers find food for them.

11 **Read the answers, and write the questions in your notebook.** 📖 ✏️

1 It is a dangerous place at night.

2 Rattlesnakes eat small animals like grasshopper mice.

3 Because if a grasshopper mouse becomes too cold and wet, it can die.

4 The grasshopper mouse must dry his fur very quickly.

12 **Write some instructions in your notebook to help the grasshopper mouse survive.** ✏️ ❓

1. Sleep in the day . . .

13 Choose the correct words, and write the full sentences in your notebook.

1 The **bigger** / **biggest** dangers to the grasshopper mouse are the Harris hawks, which are very clever birds.

2 Harris hawks can see eight times **better** / **best** than a human.

3 Luckily, the mouse finds a **safe** / **safest** place inside the bones of a dead animal.

4 Then, this **brave** / **braver** little survivor finds his way back home.

14 Listen to Chapter Seven. Describe how the Harris hawk hunts the grasshopper mouse. What does the grasshopper mouse do?

*To complete this activity, listen to track 8 of the audio download available at www.ladybirdeducation.co.uk

15 **Read the questions. Write the answers in full sentences in your notebook, using the words in the box.** 📖 🖊

> food insects nose
> trails tongue savanna

1 Where do sengis live?

2 Why are they called "elephant shrews"?

3 When do the babies hide?

4 How do the sengi mothers find food?

5 What do sengis eat?

6 How does the monitor lizard smell the sengi?

16 **Talk to a friend about the animals below.** 💬

The monitor lizard lives in a termites' nest.

17 Complete the sentences using words from Chapter Nine. Write full sentences in your notebook.

1 The young sengi soon learns it is quicker to use the . . .

2 She also learns to . . . the trails.

3 Elephants often make the trails . . . again.

4 Luckily for the sengi, thousands of . . . beetles arrive in minutes.

18 Write the answers to the questions in your notebook.

1 What do the dung beetles make with the dung?

2 How do they take them home?

3 Why do the beetles need dung?

4 How far away can dung beetles smell dung?

19 Complete the text using the words in the box. Write the full text in your notebook. 📖 ✏️ ✦

are	begin	burned
can run	do not survive	has to
have survived	have seen	looks

The wildebeest suddenly [1] . . . to run because they [2] . . . frightened. The wildebeest [3] . . . fire. Every year, there are large fires in the dry savanna. Sadly, many small animals [4] . . . . The sengi [5] . . . fast to escape the fire, but she [6] . . . leave the trail.

After the fire, the savanna [7] . . . very different. Luckily, the dry grass [8] . . . so quickly that the sengi trails [9] . . . .

20 In your notebook, write a news story about a fire in the savanna. ✏️ ❓

FIRE IN THE SAVANNA!

Yesterday, there was a large fire in the savanna!

21 Read the sentences. Choose the correct animals, and write them in your notebook. 📖 ✏️ 🗨️

chipmunk   grasshopper   sengi

mouse

1 Rattlesnakes and Harris hawks hunt it.

2 Monitor lizards hunt it.

3 Great horned owls hunt it.

22 Ask and answer the questions with a friend, using the words in the box. 🗨️

amazing   bigger   brave and clever   survive   weather

1 What is it important for little survivors to learn to do?

2 Which animals are dangerous to the little survivors?

3 What other things can be dangerous in their habitats?

4 What do these little survivors do that is the same? What do they do that is different?

Project

23 In this book, you read about these "little survivors".

chipmunk   grasshopper mouse   sengi

Find out more about a little survivor in your country. Work in a group to make a presentation about it. Include the information below:

- What is the animal called?

- Where does it live?

- How big is it?

- What does it eat?

- What does it do?

Glossary

acorn *(noun)*
a small, brown nut that falls from a tree

amazing *(adjective)*
Something that makes you feel surprised and happy is *amazing*.

bone *(noun)*
the hard parts inside the body of a human or an animal

burrow *(noun)*
an underground hole made by animals (e.g. rabbits) to live in

cheek *(noun)*
either side of the face under the eyes

clear *(adjective)*
nothing in the way

clear *(verb)*
to move things out of the way

dung *(noun)*
what comes out of an animal after food has gone through its body

fur *(noun)*
thick, soft hair on an animal's body

habitat *(noun)*
a place where an animal or plant is usually found

hibernate *(verb)*
to spend the winter sleeping

hunt *(verb)*
to follow and catch animals for food

nest *(noun)*
a thing that some animals build, often made with sticks and dry grass

protect *(verb)*
to stop anything bad happening to someone or something

season *(noun)*
a time in the year

survive *(verb)*
to continue to live

survivor *(noun)*
someone or something
that does not die

termite *(noun)*
A small insect that
lives in a group. Some
termites eat wood.

tongue *(noun)*
the soft part that moves
around inside the
mouth, which is used
for tasting

trail *(noun)*
a small path used
by animals

underground
(adjective)
under the ground

venom *(noun)*
something dangerous
inside some animals
(e.g. spiders, snakes,
scorpions), which
comes out when they
attack something

venomous *(adjective)*
something with venom
in it

whiskers *(noun)*
long hairs that some
animals have on the
sides of their faces, near
their mouths